THE MEMOIRS OF
SHERLOCK HOLMES

THE MEMOIRS OF SHERLOCK HOLMES

Arthur Conan Doyle

An imprint of Om Books International

Reprinted in 2020

Om KIDZ | Om Books International

Corporate & Editorial Office
A-12, Sector 64, Noida 201 301
Uttar Pradesh, India
Phone: +91 120 477 4100
Email: editorial@ombooks.com
Website: www.ombooksinternational.com

Sales Office
107, Ansari Road, Darya Ganj
New Delhi 110 002, India
Phone: +91 11 4000 9000
Email: sales@ombooks.com
Website: www.ombooks.com

Retold by Swayam Ganguly

ISBN: 978-93-5276-115-9

Printed in India

10 9 8 7 6 5 4 3 2

Contents

Chapter One

The Crooked Man

One summer night, after an exhaustive day at work, I was smoking my pipe and reading a novel before retiring to bed. Suddenly, I heard the clang of the doorbell. To my astonishment, it was Sherlock Holmes standing at my door step.

"I hope my visit at this hour of the day is not intruding, Watson," he enquired. "May I stay here for tonight?"

"With pleasure," I replied. Holmes sat across me silently and I knew that something really important must have brought him to my place so late at night. I waited patiently for him to speak.

"Presently, I'm in the midst of a rather difficult case. Will it be possible for you to accompany me to Aldershot tomorrow?" Holmes asked.

"I'd be delighted," I replied.

"That's good. Now, if you are not too sleepy, perhaps you'd like to know the details."

"I was sleepy before you arrived, but I'm wide awake now!"

"The case involves the supposed murder of Colonel Barclay, of the Royal Munsters, at Aldershot."

"I haven't heard anything about it, yet."

"These facts are just two days old, Watson," Holmes replied.

"The Royal Munsters is considered as one of the most famous Irish regiments in the British Army. James Barclay, a very brave man, was commanding this regiment till Monday night.

"When he was a sergeant, Colonel Barclay married Miss Nancy Devoy. She was the daughter of a former sergeant in the same corps.

Nancy Devoy was a strikingly beautiful woman and even now, after thirty years of marriage, has a queenly appearance. Major Murphy, who provided me with these facts, assured me that there was no misunderstanding between the Colonel and his wife. Murphy, in fact, stressed upon the fact that Barclay's devotion to his wife was greater than his wife's devotion to him. If she was absent for even a day, it made Barclay very uneasy.

"Although Nancy was faithful and devoted, she seemed less affectionate in comparison to him. Everyone in the regiment agreed that they were a happy middle-aged couple. Therefore, when the tragedy occurred, it took everyone by surprise. There were, however, incidences when the Colonel demonstrated traces of violence and cruelty in his behavior. Occasionally, his attitude also showed signs of depression. He would be smiling one moment, and then turn very gloomy at the very next moment. This gloomy mood would then prevail for days on end.

"The Colonel resided in a villa named Lachine, next to the army camp. This house boasted of its own grounds. A coachman and two maids who worked there made up for the staff. The Barclays were a childless couple.

"Now, Watson, let me recall the events at Lachine on the evening of last Monday between nine and ten.

"Mrs. Barclay was an active member of an NGO committed to providing basic needs to the poor. At eight the same evening, she had attended a meeting there. The coachman had overheard her assuring her husband before leaving that she would return early. Mrs. Barclay then sent for Miss Morrison, a young lady residing in the next villa, and the two of them set off for the meeting. The meeting lasted for forty minutes and Mrs. Barclay returned home at quarter-past nine, after having dropped Miss Morrison at her residence.

"A room in Lachine serves as the morning room. It faces the road and opens out to the lawn thanks to a large sliding door made of glass. The lawn is approximately thirty yards across and is separated from the highway only by a low wall with an iron rail above it. Mrs. Barclay entered this very room after she returned from her meeting.

"It was a rarity for this room to be used in the evening but Mrs. Barclay lit the lamp personally and then asked the housemaid, Jane Stewart, to fetch her a cup of tea. This was a rather unusual request from her. The Colonel had been seated in the dining room and joined his wife in the morning room after learning of her arrival. Their coachman had spotted him cross the hallway and enter the room. After that day he was never seen alive.

"Her maid prepared the tea in ten minutes, but when she approached the door, she was surprised to hear the angry voices of her master

and mistress. When she did not get a response after knocking the door, she tried the door handle only to discover that it was locked from the inside. The maid ran downstairs to inform the cook and the two women came up to the hall, accompanied by the coachman. They listened to the argument from outside.

"They could not make out what Barclay was saying as his statements were low, brief and crisp but they could easily hear what their mistress was saying, especially when she raised her voice. 'You coward!' she repeated again and again. 'There is nothing that can be done now! Give me back my life! I do not wish to live with you ever again. You coward! You coward!'

"All of a sudden, the man let out a dreadful cry, followed by a loud crash and a piercing scream from the woman. The coachman tried to force open the door immediately but failed and the maids were too stunned to offer him any help. So, he ran to the lawn and entered the room, thanks to an open French window. He noticed that his mistress had fainted on the couch. He saw his master lying on the ground with his feet tilted over the side of an armchair. The poor soldier was lying in a pool of his own blood. Dead to the world!

"The initial thought of the coachman was to open the door. But he failed to find the key anywhere. So, he exited the room through the window and later returned with a policeman and a doctor. The lady, against, whom the strongest suspicion rested, was removed from the room. She was still in a state of shock. The Colonel's dead body was then placed on the sofa and a careful examination of the crime scene was carried out.

"Death had been caused by injuries to the back of the head. A severe blow from a blunt weapon had caused these injuries. It was easy to guess which weapon had been used as a strange club rested next to the body on the floor.

This was made of hard carved wood and had a bone handle. The police didn't find any other important clue in the room. But the key was missing and couldn't be located anywhere in the room; it was not on the dead body or with Mrs. Barclay.

"At Major Murphy's request, I went down to Aldershot on Tuesday morning to help the police. I gathered from the police that Miss Morrison had found the lady to be fine when she was with her. After having gathered the facts, I tried to analyse them. Among them, the disappearance of the door key is the most unusual and suggests that a third party must have entered the room. That third person could have only entered through the window and so, I examined the lawn carefully to discover the traces of this mysterious person. I did find the traces but they were very different from what I had expected them to be. I was convinced now that a man did enter the room and had

crossed the lawn from the road to do so. Five clear marks of his footprints suggested this. But what surprised me were the footprints of this man's companion," Holmes paused.

"Companion?"

"An animal, in fact," Holmes replied. They were not of a dog, a cat or a monkey that we are familiar with. This animal has a long body with rather short legs according to the reconstruction I have arrived at from its measurements. It can run up a curtain and is a carnivore.

"How on earth do you know that, Holmes?"

"Well, it did run up the curtain. There was a canary's cage hanging on the window and the creature tried to get at the bird," Holmes explained.

"What does that have to do with the crime?"

"I'm not very sure about that just yet," Holmes confessed.

"Your discoveries make the matter even more mysterious," I exclaimed.

"Yes. So, I thought of some other points as well. Mrs. Barclay was happy with her husband when she exited the house at seven thirty. When she returned, she had instantly gone to the morning room where it was least likely for her husband to be present. To calm herself down, she had asked for some tea. Then, before the tea arrived, her husband did, and a violent argument ensued. Hence, something must have occurred between half-past seven and nine o'clock that had completely altered Mrs. Barclay's feelings towards her husband. Now, Miss Morrison had been with the lady for this entire period. It is certain that she knows everything about this episode despite her denial. So what did I do, Watson? I simply visited Miss Morrison and told her that if she did not reveal the truth, her dear friend Mrs. Barclay would be arrested.

" 'I promised my dear friend that I would speak nothing about the matter,' Miss Morrison said, after a moment's hesitation. 'However, if she is not able to tell you the truth, then I must tell you what took place on Monday evening. We were on our way home from the meeting and it was quarter to nine. As we passed through Hudson Street, I saw a man approaching us. He had a very bent back and a box like thing was slung over one of his shoulders. He walked with a bowed head and bent knees. As we passed him, he raised his face to look at us. Then, he stopped and screamed out in a deathly voice, "My God, it's Nancy!" Mrs. Barclay turned as pale as death! I was about to call for the police, but to my sheer surprise, she spoke rather nicely to the strange man.

" ' "I thought you'd been dead these thirty years, Henry," she said, in a quivering voice.

" ' "I thought the same too," he said in a dark tone that was quite awful to hear. He had a face that was dark, wrinkled and scary. I left the two of them alone on Mrs. Barclay's request and

walked a little further away. They spoke for a
few minutes and then I saw her walking down
the street towards me, eyes blazing with rage.
The crippled man was standing by the lamp
post, shaking his head in anger. She didn't utter
a word till we were at my door, where she held
me by the hand and begged me not to reveal to
anyone what I had just witnessed. This is the
complete truth!'

"Watson, this crippled man was the missing
piece in the puzzle," Holmes stated. "My next
move was to locate this man and it was not
difficult to find a person with his description.
However, I still spent a day searching for him
and managed to locate him today evening. The
man goes by the name of Henry Wood and
lives in Hudson Street, although he has been
there just five days. His landlady informed me
that he is a magician and a performer by trade.
He carries a creature with him in a box that
he uses in some of his tricks and the landlady

says she has never seen a creature like that in her life. Watson, he is the only person who can reconstruct the events that occurred in the room that day."

"You plan to ask him, Holmes?"

"Certainly, will you accompany me tomorrow?"

We reached Hudson Street at noon the very next day and in a moment, were face to face with the man we had come to meet. He sat huddled up in his chair, and even though he had a worn-out face now, I could make out that he had been a handsome man in his youth. Although he did seem suspicious, he motioned us to be seated.

"Mr. Henry Wood," Holmes began gently, "I have come to speak to you about Colonel Barclay's death."

"What do I know about that?" the man questioned.

"Your old friend, Mrs. Barclay, will be charged for murder unless things are cleared up," Holmes stated gravely. The man pondered for some time and then declared, "Upon my word, she is innocent!"

"It is you who are guilty then?"

"No!"

"Then who killed Colonel James Barclay?" Holmes demanded.

"Destiny! It was destiny that killed him. But keep in mind that I wish I had killed him with my bare hands long ago. But the fact is that his guilty conscience took his life. Let me tell you the full story.

"You see me now, with my back like the hump of a camel. But there was a time when Corporal Henry Wood was the smartest soldier in the 117th Foot. We were stationed in India then at a place we'll call Bhurtee. Barclay was the sergeant and one of the two men who were in love with Nancy Devoy, daughter of the former sergeant, and the most beautiful girl in the regiment. But Nancy loved only one man and although you'll laugh when you look at me now, it was me that she loved.

"Ironically, she loved me for my good looks back then. Her father wanted her to marry Barclay as he was a better educated man than me and was on the verge of a promotion. But Nancy was fiercely loyal to me and refused to marry Barclay. The Mutiny broke out just then and all hell broke loose in the entire country. We were all trapped in Bhurtee, with our womenfolk and children, and ten thousand rebel soldiers had surrounded us.

"During the second week of the Mutiny, we realized that our only chance of survival lay in communicating with General Neill's column that was moving up the country. It was our only chance as we could not hope to fight our way through ten thousand rebels with women and children with us. I volunteered to step out and touch base with General Neill's column. My offer was accepted and I discussed my escape

route with Sergeant Barclay, as he knew the route better than any other soldier. He drew up a route for me and I departed at ten o' clock that night.

"My route ran down a dried-up watercourse and we hoped that it would conceal me from the enemies. But I ran straight into six of the rebels as I made my way around the watercourse. Our enemies were waiting for me in the dark and I was captured. My hands and feet were bound instantly. But the real damage was not to my body but to my heart. From whatever I could understand from the rebels' conversation, it was apparent that Sergeant Barclay had betrayed me into the hands of the enemy. General Neill relieved Bhurtee the very next day, but the rebels left with me and I never saw a white face for as long as five years. I was tortured mercilessly in their retreat and you can see the state in which they left me.

"I did manage to escape after a while and wandered about for many years. At last, I

returned to Punjab, lived among the natives and learnt magic tricks to make a living. I could certainly not return to England as a cripple and live among my family and friends. Even my thirst for revenge was not strong enough for me to do that. It was better that Nancy and my old friends thought that Henry Wood had died with a straight back than see him live with a bent back. Everyone thought that I was a dead man.

"I received news that Barclay had married Nancy and had received a promotion in the regiment. But even that could not provoke me to reveal the truth. But when one does get old, there is a strong yearning to return home. For years, the craving to see the bright green fields of England had been dominating my senses. So, I decided to visit England before I died. I saved enough to make the trip to England and arrived here."

"Your narrative is most interesting indeed," Holmes commented. "I am aware of your

meeting with Mrs. Barclay and the fact that the two of you recognized each other. So, if I am correct, you followed her home and watched the argument she had with her husband through the open window. You could not control your own feelings after that and you ran across the lawn to break into the room!"

"Yes, sir," Henry Wood replied. "Barclay was so shocked to see me that he doubled over and fell right on his head. But he was a dead man even before he hit the floor. The very sight of me was like a bullet running straight through his guilty heart."

"What happened after that?"

"Nancy fainted, and I caught the key of the door from her hand as she fell. I wanted to unlock the door and fetch help. But as I was doing so, a sudden thought struck my head. What if they thought I was guilty of murder and arrested me? So, in my haste, I slipped the key into my pocket and as I chased Teddy, who

had run up a curtain, I also dropped my stick. I ran off as fast as I could after that."

"Who's Teddy?" Holmes inquired.

Henry Wood bent down and opened the box that was lying at the corner of the room. A beautiful, reddish-brown creature slipped out instantly. It had short legs and was thin and lithe. It also had a thin, long nose and the most beautiful red eyes I ever saw in an animal head. "Why, it's a mongoose!" I exclaimed.

"Yes," Wood replied. "That's Teddy, the snake-catcher."

"We might visit you again, Mr. Wood, if Mrs. Barclay is in serious trouble," Holmes said as he got up.

"I'd come forward instantly in that case," Wood promised.

"Yes, but if not, there is no need for raking up such a scandal against a dead man," Holmes replied. "Even though he has acted in the most cunning and vile manner possible, Mr. Wood, at

least you have the satisfaction of knowing that he has suffered for thirty years with a guilty conscience for this misdeed. Ah, I can see Major Murphy on the other side of the street. We shall get to know the latest events since yesterday from him. Goodbye Wood!"

We caught up with the Major before he had turned the corner.

"There you are, Holmes," he stated. "You've heard I suppose?"

"What?"

"The inquest just got over. According to the medical evidence, death was caused by apoplexy. It was a simple case after all!"

"Of course it was," Holmes said with a smile. "Come, Watson. I don't think we are needed in Aldershot anymore!"

Chapter Two

The "Gloria Scott"

"I have some papers with me," Holmes said to me as we sat beside the fire one winter night. "You should take a look at these papers, Watson. These are the documents of the extraordinary case of the Gloria Scott, and this is the message which killed Justice Trevor when he read it."

I took the short note written upon a half sheet of grey paper and read it.

"The supply of game for London is going steadily up. Head-keeper Hudson, we believe, has been now told to receive all orders for fly-paper and for preservation of your hen-pheasant's life."

I stared at Holmes after reading this strange message and saw him laughing. "You do look a little surprised, Watson," he said.

"I cannot fathom how such a message can convey horror to someone," I said.

"True. But the fact is that the reader, a fine, robust old man, died after reading it."

"That is surprising!"

Holmes leaned forward in his armchair and spread out the document upon his knees. "I never mentioned Victor Trevor to you?" he enquired. "He was the only friend I made during my two years at college. He was a hearty chap, full of energy and spirit. Once, I was invited by him to spend a month long vacation at his father's place at Donnithorpe, Norfolk. Donnithorpe is a small town just to the north of Langmere, in the country of the Broads.

"It was a wide-spread, old-fashioned house with an oak-beamed brick building. It boasted of a big garden, a good fishing pond, a backyard

with hens and ducks, and a small library. My friend's father was a widower and Trevor was the only son. Trevor was well traveled and was a broad, burly man with curly hair. He had a rough, brown face with blue eyes. Trevor was renowned as a kind person who did a lot of charity work."

"The three of us were sitting and chatting after dinner one day when young Trevor began praising my habits of observation and inference that he so admired. His old man thought he was exaggerating and laughed.

"'I'm an excellent subject, Mr. Holmes,' he said in jest. 'What can you say just by observing me now?'

"'I'm afraid there's not much to say,' I replied. 'But it seems that you have lived in fear of some personal attack within the past twelve months.'

"Watson, the laugh died on his lips and he stared at me open-mouthed.

" 'Well, that's the truth,' he confessed. 'I've been on the guard always when it comes to the local poaching gang. But I'm clueless how you did that.'

" 'You possess a rather handsome stick,' I replied. 'It is very new. But you have converted it into an excellent weapon by boring its head and by pouring melted lead into the hole. Such precautions are unnecessary unless there is some danger or fear.'

" 'Is there anything else?', he asked smilingly.

" 'You have boxed a lot in your youth.'

" 'How did you know that?'

" 'From the shape of your ears. They have a strange flattening and thickening that marks the boxing man.'

" 'Anything else?'

" 'Well, you have done a lot of digging.'

" 'Yes, made all my money at the gold fields.'

" 'You have also been to New Zealand and Japan sometime.'

" 'True.'

" 'You also knew someone whose initials were J.A. Later, you were in a hurry to forget this man entirely.'

"Mr. Trevor rose slowly, fixing his large, blue eyes on me in a wild stare. Then, he fainted suddenly. Both his son and I were shocked. We immediately revived him by sprinkling water on his face. He gave a couple of gasps and then sat up.

" 'Ah, my boys,' he said with a forced smile, 'I hope I haven't scared you. I might look strong but there exists a weak place in my heart. I am unaware how you managed to do this, Mr. Holmes, but I can safely say that all the detectives in the world will appear nothing when compared to you.'

"Watson, that recommendation was the first thing that made me feel confident enough to pursue my hobby as a career. But at that time, all that concerned me was Trevor Senior's health.

" 'I hope I haven't said anything that caused you pain?' I said.

" 'Well, you certainly took me back to my past. How did you know?' he said with a look of terror.

" 'Simple. J.A. had been tattooed in the bend of your elbow. The letters are still readable although blurred, but it was clear that an attempt had been made to remove them.'

" 'Oh, what an eye you have,' he marveled with a sigh of relief. 'But let us not talk about the past. What's gone is gone!'

"But from that day onwards, there was always a touch of suspicion in Mr. Trevor's behavior towards me. I decided to cut short my visit as my presence was making him uneasy. But an important incident occurred the same day, before I left. That afternoon, as the three of us were relaxing in the lawn, a small, old fellow with a limp, arrived. He was dressed in an open jacket, a red and black check shirt, dungaree

trousers and old, heavy boots. His face was thin, brown and cunning. His smile displayed his yellow teeth and his crinkled hands proved that he had been a sailor. Mr. Trevor gasped when he saw this man.

" 'What can I do for you?' he asked.

" 'You don't know me?' the sailor asked him with a sinister smile.

" 'Oh lord, it is surely Hudson,' Mr. Trevor said in surprise.

" 'Hudson it is sir,' the seaman exclaimed. 'Why, I haven't seen you for thirty years. Now here you are in your fine house, and I still don't have any money to buy food.'

" 'You will find that I haven't forgotten the old times,' Mr. Trevor cried and approached the sailor. 'Go to the kitchen,' he whispered. 'You will find food and drink there. I shall also get you a job.'

" 'Thank you sir,' the sailor replied, touching his forelock. 'That's what I need and I thought I'd get it with either Mr. Beddoes or you.'

" 'You know where Mr. Beddoes is?' Mr. Trevor exclaimed.

" 'Of course, Sir. I know where all my old friends are,' the sailor replied with a menacing smile. Both of them left for the kitchen and an hour later, when we entered the house, we discovered him lying drunk upon the dining room sofa. That entire incident left an ugly mark on my mind, and I happily left for London. I had almost forgotten about the entire episode till one day, I received a telegram from my friend urging me to return to Donnithorpe, urgently. He said he greatly needed my assistance and advice. I left immediately.

"When I met my friend at the station, I saw that he was not in good health. He had become thin and his usual cheerfulness was missing. 'Father is dying!' were his first words.

" 'Impossible!' I exclaimed. 'What happened?'

" 'Apoplexy. Nervous shock, I fear we won't find him alive.'

"The unexpected news stunned me and I asked him for the reason.

" 'Do you recall that strange man who visited us just before you left?'

" 'Of course.'

" 'We haven't had a moment's peace ever since that horrible man arrived. I've never seen my father so scared of anyone.'

" 'What kind of power does he hold over your father?'

" 'I'd give anything in the world to find that out. I'm glad you've arrived now, Holmes. There is no other man that I'd trust and I know that your advice will be the best.'

"As we rushed to the house, Trevor gave me the details.

" 'That fellow was appointed gardener by my father. Then, as if the act did not satisfy him, he was promoted to butler. Very soon, he developed airs as if he owned the house itself. He did whatever he wished and sneered at my father all the time. I was furious but father never lost his temper with him. Things turned from bad to worse as this man called Hudson became more and more rude. Then, one day, he said something unpardonable to father. I could not take it anymore and pushed him out of the room. He left with a threatening look. I refused when father asked me to apologize to Hudson. My father shut himself up in his room after that and I saw him writing down something from the window. Hudson informed us that very evening that he was leaving us. He said he'd had enough of Norfolk and would visit Mr. Beddoes in Hampshire. "He'll be as happy to see me as you were, Mr. Trevor."

" 'My father turned pale and turned to me with a look that suggested that I should apologize. But I turned away. Hudson left and my father has been extremely nervous since then. Yesterday evening, a letter bearing the Fordingbridge postmark arrived for him. After

reading the letter, father clapped his hands to his head and paced the room. Then, he had a stroke and fell down. Dr. Fordham arrived soon and we put him to bed in an unconscious state.'

" 'That's terrible news, Trevor!' I cried. 'What were the contents of this letter?'

"We arrived at the house just then, and a servant rushed out to inform us that Trevor Senior had passed away. We met the doctor as we were rushing inside, who informed us that Trevor Senior had died as soon as Trevor had left the house.

" 'Was there any message he had for me?' Trevor enquired.

" 'He just said that the papers were in the back drawer of the Japanese cabinet,' the doctor replied.

"Trevor accompanied the doctor, while I remained in the study, trying to think over what had happened. I remembered that Fordingham was located in Hampshire and that Mr. Beddoes

"The supply of game for London is going steadliy up. Head-keeper Hudson,we believe,hab been now told to receive all orders for fly-paper and for preservation of your hen-pheasant's life."

also lived in Hampshire. The letter could have come from either Hudson or Mr. Beddoes as a warning for Trevor Senior. But how could Trevor dismiss this letter as unimportant? He must have misread it and if so, it must have been written in code language that Trevor could not comprehend. As I thought about all this, Trevor arrived, pale yet calm, with these very papers that I'm holding right now.

"The letter that he handed me said, 'The supply of game for London is going steadily up. Head-keeper Hudson, we believe, has been now told to receive all orders for fly-paper and for preservation of your hen-pheasant's life.'

"Watson, I was indeed surprised when I first read this message. Then, I realized that it must have some secret meaning and reread it carefully. I tried arranging the words, tried them backwards and even read it with alternate words. But it still remained a mystery! Then, I got it all of a sudden! You see, every third

word, beginning with the first, would convey the message that would give old Trevor a shock. The message was nothing but a warning!

" 'The game is up. Hudson has told all. Fly for your life.'

"Victor Trevor was trembling. 'I suppose it must be that. Why, it must have been worse than death itself as it suggests disgrace. But what do the words 'head-keepers' and 'hen-pheasants' mean?'

" 'It's not related to the message, but it gives an insight to the sender. He uses the words 'game' and 'hen-pheasant,' etc. Do you have Any idea about Beddoes?'

" 'Yes, now I remember. Father used to receive an invitation from him to go shooting every autumn.'

" 'We now need to discover what the secret was, Trevor.'

" 'Alas, Holmes! I am afraid that it's a secret full of sin and shame. But there cannot be any secrets from you. Here is my father's statement written for me. They are the details of the travel on the ship called *Gloria Scott,* from the day she left Falmouth on the 8th of October, 1855, to her end on November 6th. The letter runs thus:

"'My dear, dear son, now that the secret is in the open, let me write to you as an honest and truthful man should. I am very sorry to have kept this secret from you. But I'd rather you learn about it from me than from someone else. I hope you will forgive me, dear son. My name is not Trevor! My real name is James Armitage. Under this name, I joined a London banking-house and under this very name, I was arrested for breaking the laws of my country. I was sentenced to transportation under the name of Armitage.

" 'But let me make it clear that I did not steal, son. I just took some money to clear off my debts and I intended to replace the money without anyone coming to know about it. But as luck would have it, my boss discovered the theft before I could replace the money. I was accused, convicted and found myself bound in chains with thirty-seven other convicts in a ship called Gloria Scott bound for Australia. She was a five-hundred ton boat, carrying twenty-six crew members, eighteen soldiers, a captain, three mates, a chaplain, a doctor, four warders and a hundred prisoners. One night, a few prisoners planned their escape through whispered messages.

" 'I decided to join them when I learnt of their plan. We managed to capture some of the guns and bombs but the doctor saw the hidden pistols under the bunk when he came to attend to a prisoner. We gagged and tied him on the bed. Then, we attacked. We killed the two sentries first, and then the soldiers and the mates were gunned down. Only the doctor and the captain remained. Most of us did not want to kill them as they were unarmed but two of

us insisted that they had to be killed. We were divided and the two men offered a solution. We could take the boats and leave first if we did not want to be a part of the killing. They would join us after killing the captain and the doctor. We agreed and left. But when we were rowing our boat away from the ship, the strangest thing happened.

" 'There was a loud explosion on the ship followed by a puff of smoke. Then, the ship disappeared completely. Instantly, we turned around towards the ship to look for survivors. We reached the place where the ship had been after a lengthy hour and thought we were too late to save anyone. As we turned away, we heard a cry of anguish. We spotted a man lying on a piece of wood a little further away. We pulled the burned man on the boat and learnt that he was a young seaman named Hudson. Through him we came to know that as the two factions had fought, one of the seamen had

thrown a burning match on a barrel of oil. This had caused the explosion.

" 'So, this is the horrible business which I was a part of, dear boy. We were picked up the next day by the ship, Hotspur, bound for Australia. The captain believed us to be the survivors of a sunk passenger ship. We reached Sydney, where my prison-mate Evans and I changed our names. We started work at the digging fields and made money. We lived a peaceful and normal life for more than twenty years, secure in the knowledge that our dark past had been buried. And then, one day, this Hudson returns, threatening to reveal everything.'

"That was the dramatic story, Watson. Trevor was heartbroken. After the letter of warning was written, nothing was heard of Hudson or Beddoes. It seemed they had disappeared from the face of the earth. No complaint had been lodged with the police either."

Chapter Three

The Musgrave Ritual

When Watson visited Sherlock Holmes at his residence in Baker Street one day, he found him in a mood for narrating one of his old adventures.

Holmes initiated the conversation by saying, "Watson, when I was in London, I used to study at the University. Cases came my way now and then as fellow students became aware about me and my methods. The Musgrave Ritual was one such case."

"Reginald Musgrave attended the same college as me. He was thin, large eyed, high-nosed, and an extremely aristocratic type. He

is the heir of one of the oldest families in the kingdom, in western Sussex, where the Manor House of Hurlstone is arguably the oldest building in the county. I did not see Reginald for four years after the University days, till he chose to arrive at my house one day."

" 'How are you Musgrave?' I enquired.

" 'I have been managing the Hurlstone estates since my father's death two years ago,' he informed me. 'You have chosen to be a detective then, Holmes?'

"Yes," I replied.

"That is delightful to hear, as your advice would greatly help me in my current state. Something strange is going on at Hurlstone and the police have failed to get to the bottom of this extraordinary matter."

"Let me have the details, please," I exclaimed, quite excited.

So, Reginald Musgrave began to recount his strange story.

"You must be aware, Holmes, that I have many servants at Hurlstone even though I am a bachelor. It is an old place after all, and needs looking after. There are eight maids, a cook, a butler, two footmen and a boy. Brunton, the butler, has served us the longest, having been employed by my father. Brunton is a handsome man about forty years of age. He has displayed great energy and character over the years to make himself indispensable. Brunton could have easily gone and served at a better position, but I think he is comfortable with us. His one fault is his flirtatious nature, though.

"A couple of months ago, he was engaged to marry Rachel Howells, the second housemaid. But he left her after meeting Janet Tregellis, the daughter of the head game-keeper. Rachel was a good, chirpy girl. She had a brain fever after this incident and moves around the house now as a shadow of her former self or so it was until yesterday. That was the first drama at

Hurlstone. The second act was the disgrace and dismissal of Brunton. They say curiosity killed the cat! It was similar in Brunton's case as he was curious about everything. His intelligence was his downfall.

"I discovered I could not sleep last Thursday night. At two in the morning, I lit a candle to read a novel. But as the book was in the billiard room, I slipped on my dressing gown and went to fetch it. I descended the stairs to cross the passage that also leads to the library. But to my amazement, I saw a shimmer of light from the open door of the library. I fully remembered that I had extinguished the lamp and shut the library door before retiring to bed. My first thought was that a thief had broken in. Trophies of old weapons adorn the walls at the Hurlstone corridors and I picked up a battle-axe. I walked on tiptoe and peered through the open door."

" 'Brunton, the butler was in the library. He was seated and fully dressed, studying

something like a map spread upon his knees. I was shocked but my shock turned to anger when he rose to walk across the room and unlock a drawer. He fished out a paper from it and returned to his seat. Flattening the paper on the table, he began to study it with immense concentration. I was enraged when I saw him viewing our family documents without permission. I stepped forward and Brunton jumped to his feet when he spotted me. His face was full of fear."

" ' "So!" "This is how you repay the trust that we have put in you, Brunton. You shall leave my service tomorrow."

" 'Brunton bowed with a look of disappointment and exited without a word. I inspected what he had been studying and was surprised to find that it was nothing important at all. It was merely a copy of the questions and answers about a strange old observance called the Musgrave Ritual. This is a peculiar

ceremony observed by our family, which each Musgrave adult has to observe when he comes of age. I relocked the drawer and turned to see that the butler had returned.'

" ' "Mr. Musgrave, sir," he exclaimed in tears, 'there's no way for me to bear this disgrace. I'd rather kill myself. I beg you, if you cannot keep me, let me leave in a month by giving you notice, as if I was doing it of my own free will. I can't bear being thrown out like this, please, Mr. Musgrave."

" ' "You don't deserve such treatment, Brunton," I replied. "But as you have been with the family for a long time, I do not wish to bring public disgrace upon you. But a month is too long a notice period for you. Leave in a week."

" 'Brunton pleaded with me to be allowed to stay for a fortnight but I refused to relent and he left for his rooms like a broken man. For two days after this, Brunton was extremely attentive with his duties. But he did not show

75

up on the third day, after breakfast, to receive his orders for the day, as custom demanded. I met Rachel Howells, the maid, after I exited the dining room. She looked very pale as she was still recovering from her illness. I asked her to retire to bed and return when she was strong enough to work. She gave me a strange look and replied that she was strong enough to work.'

" ' "We will see what the doctor has to say about that," I replied. "Now stop work and when you go downstairs, tell Brunton I wish to see him."

" ' "The butler has left, sir," she informed me.

" ' "Where?" I asked.

" ' "He is gone! He is not there in his room. No one has seen him. Yes, he is gone!" She fell back against the wall, laughing hysterically. Immediately, I summoned for help. When the girl was being taken to her room, I enquired about Brunton. It was certain that he had left without a doubt as his bed had not been slept in and no one had seen him. But how he could have left the house was a mystery as all the doors and windows were locked. His belongings like his clothes, watch and money were still in the room but his black suit, which he normally wore, was gone. So were his slippers. But where the butler had gone in the night still remained a mystery. Searching the house and calling the local police for help did not yield any result.

" 'Rachel Howell had been so sick for two days that a nurse had to be employed all night to take care of her. On the third night, after Brunton had disappeared, this nurse had dozed off in her armchair, seeing her patient sleep peacefully. When the nurse woke up in the morning, her patient had disappeared too. The window was open! I was aroused immediately and set off to look for the girl with two footmen. We followed her footmarks across the lawn to the edge of the lake. We thought she had flung herself into the eight feet deep lake but could not find her body. But we did find an unexpected object in the form of a linen bag that had a mass of rusted and discoloured metal. There was no sign of either Rachel Howells or Richard Brunton.'

" 'I must see that paper the butler was so interested in,' I demanded.

" 'This ritual of ours is quite an absurd business,' he replied. 'I have a copy of the questions and answers right here if you want to see them.'

"Watson, these are the questions," Holmes stated, as he took out a piece of paper from his drawer. "Let me read the questions and answers aloud to you.

" 'Whose was it?'
" 'His who is gone.'
" 'Who shall have it?'
" 'He who will come.'
" 'Where was the sun?'
" 'Over the oak.'
" 'Where was the shadow?'

" 'Under the elm.'

" 'How was it stepped?'

" 'North by ten and by ten, east by five and by five, south by two and by two, west by one and by one, and so under.'

" 'There is no date to be found on the original,' Musgrave remarked.

" 'That might help us solve the mystery. Your butler appears to have been a rather clever man, Musgrave.'

" 'How is that?,' Musgrave enquired. 'The paper seems perfectly useless to me.'

" 'It does seem rather useful to me, and I think Brunton felt the same way.'

" 'But what is his connection with our old family ritual? Whatever does this ritual mean?'

" 'The answer to this lies at Hurlstone itself,' I replied.

"I visited Hurlstone that afternoon. It is built L shaped, the long arm constituting the more modern portion and the shorter arm

being the older one. The date '1607' is carved on the heavy outer door but experts are of the opinion that the stone-work and the beams are far older than that. The older part was used as a storage space while the family resided in the modern part. The house was ensconced in a beautiful park and a large lake. Watson, it was clear to me that only one mystery existed here instead of three separate ones. Only the Musgrave Ritual could solve this mystery! On reading the ritual, it was also clear to me that the measurements indicated a particular spot, and if that spot could be found, the secret of the Musgrave Ritual would be revealed. To begin with, two guides had been provided in the oak and the elm. A huge oak tree stood right in front of the house, upon the left hand side of the drive.

" 'That tree must have existed when your ritual was drawn up,' I mentioned to Musgrave. 'Are there any old elms?'

" 'There used to be a very old one over yonder,' he replied. 'But we cut down the stump when it was struck by lightning ten years ago,'

" 'One can see where it used to stand?'

" 'Yes!'

" 'Any other elm?'

" 'No.'

"We proceeded to the spot where the old elm had stood. It was located almost midway between the house and the oak.

" 'How high was this elm?,' I asked.

" 'Sixty-four feet.'

" 'Did your butler ever ask you this question?'

"Musgrave was surprised. 'Now that you mention it, he did enquire about the height of the elm a couple of months ago.'

"Watson, this was a welcome news, as it meant that I was on the right track. I stared up at the sun to realise that it was low in the sky. According to my calculations, it would lie just above the topmost branches of the old oak in less than an hour. One of the conditions mentioned in the ritual would be fulfilled. Then, I had to determine where the far end of the shadow of the elm would fall when the sun was just above the oak."

"That must have been difficult, Holmes, as the elm was non-existent."

"Well, not really. All I did was accompany Musgrave to his study. I tied a long string to a peg with a knot at each yard. Then, taking two lengths of a fishing rod that came precisely to six feet, I returned to the elm again with Musgrave. I attached the rod on end, marked out the direction of the shadow, and measured it. It was exactly nine feet in length!

"The calculation was simple, of course. If a rod of six feet was capable of throwing a shadow of nine feet, then a tree of sixty four feet would cast a shadow of ninety six. I carefully measured out the distance and almost reached the wall of the house in the process.

I thrust a peg into the spot and immediately spotted another mark there, possibly made by Brunton. This was my starting point and I began stepping with the help of my pocket compass. Ten steps with each foot took me parallel along the wall of the house and I marked my spot again with a peg. I went five to the east and two to the south carefully after that to arrive at the old, heavy door. Two steps to the west indicated that I was to go down the stone passage. This was the place indicated by the Musgrave Ritual!

" 'Is there a cellar below?' I cried.

" 'Yes, down here, through this door,' Musgrave replied.

"Musgrave struck a match to light a large lantern as we descended a winding, stone stair. It was clear instantly that we were not the only recent visitors here. There were a few wooden planks lying on the floor and a large, heavy flat stone stood in the middle. It had a rusted

iron ring in the centre to which a thick muffler was attached.

" 'That looks like Brunton's muffler,' Musgrave exclaimed.

"Musgrave summoned some of the county police at my suggestion. We lifted the heavy stone together after they arrived. We saw a small black hole below. A small chamber approximately seven feet deep and four feet square stared at us. A brass-bound wooden box lay in a corner, the lid open. Several old coins lay scattered over the top of the box, but it had nothing else. However, what lay beside the box stunned us all. It was a dead man wearing a black suit. Musgrave identified him as the missing butler. There was no wound on the dead man to indicate how he had met with his death.

" 'What is the meaning of all this, Holmes?' Musgrave enquired.

"I was lost in deep thought and it all came to me in the span of a few minutes. Brunton was

aware that something valuable was hidden and he had identified the place as well. He realised that the heavy stone was impossible for one person to move. He needed help and in this situation, it was better to get help from within the house rather than from outside. The housemaid had been devoted to him and so he apologized to her and asked her to help him. Together, they must have come and lifted up the stone at night. Only one person could have fitted into the hole and clearly, Brunton would have gone inside while the girl waited above. Brunton must have unlocked the box and would have handed over the contents to the girl, as the box was empty. What could have happened after that? The heavy stone would have fallen accidently upon the hole and would have trapped Brunton inside. Although, unintentional, the girl must have extracted her revenge, and would have run away with the treasure while Brunton

screamed for mercy. That explains why she had been so troubled the following morning. But what had she done with the contents of the box? Clearly, the contents must have been the old metal and pebbles that had been fished out from the lake by my client. Howells must have thrown them in there to remove all traces of her crime."

"Musgrave peered down the hole and swung his lantern. He looked very pale.

" 'These are coins of Charles the First,' he declared, amazed.

" 'It is possible that we might find something else that belongs to Charles the First,' I said excitedly, as the probable meaning of the first two questions of the Ritual suddenly dawned upon me. 'Let's have a look at that bag you got from the mere.'

"The metal had turned black and the stones appeared dull. But after I rubbed one of them on my sleeve, it glowed brightly.

" 'Keep in mind that after the king of England died, some of his followers fled the country. But they left their valuable possessions buried behind them, with the intent of returning for them when peace was restored in the land.'

" 'My ancestor, Sir Ralph Musgrave, was a great supporter of Charles I during the English Civil War,' Musgrave disclosed.

" 'Then I must congratulate you for getting these possessions and also for the Crown!'

" 'The Crown?'

" 'Yes. Remember what the Ritual says: *"Whose was it?" "His who is gone."*

That was after Charles was executed. Then, *"Who shall have it?" "He who will come."*That refers to Charles the Second.'

" 'But why didn't Charles get his crown upon his return?' Musgrave asked as he put back the Crown into its linen bag.

" 'That, my friend, is history. It is possible that the Musgrave who kept the secret died in the

interval, and the clue was left to his descendant without any explanation of the meaning. After that, it has been handed down from father to son, generation after generation, until at last, the secret chose to be revealed by a man, who lost his life in the adventure.'"

Chapter Four

The Reigate Puzzle

Colonel Hayter, my old friend, had extended an invitation to me to come and stay at his country home for a short vacation. So, last April, I left for Reigate in Surrey, accompanied by my friend Sherlock Holmes.

The evening we arrived, as we chatted with the Colonel after dinner, he spoke about a local robbery case. "Old Acton, who is the rich man of our country, had his house burgled last Sunday. There was no major damage done but the fellows haven't been arrested yet."

"No clue?" Holmes enquired.

"None as yet. The entire place had been turned upside down. But all they left with were some books, two plated candlesticks, an ivory letter-weight and a ball of wool."

"Strange things to take!" I exclaimed. All Holmes did was grunt. "The county police must have made something out of that," he remarked. "There must have been something specific the robbers had been looking for."

The next morning, it was discovered that the small problem had escalated into something bigger. The Colonel's butler rushed in during breakfast. "Have you heard the news at the Cunningham's sir?" he exclaimed.

"Burglary?" the Colonel exclaimed.

"Murder!"

"What?" the Colonel whistled. "Who's been murdered, then?"

"William the coachman, sir. Shot through the heart."

"Who killed him?"

"The burglar, sir. He ran away after that. He had just entered through the window and William spotted him. He died saving his master's property."

"When did this happen?"

"Last night, around midnight, sir."

"Mr. Cunningham will be a sad man as William was in his employ for many years and was a good servant. It looks like the work of the same villains who had broken into Acton's."

"The ones who stole that strange collection," Holmes commented thoughtfully.

"Precisely"

"Isn't it strange that a gang of burglars chose to rob two houses here instead of the city?" Holmes asked.

"Local thieves probably. It's not strange that they should pick Acton's and Cunningham's as they are the largest in this area."

"And the richest?"

"Apparently, they've had a lawsuit for several years now, and the lawsuit has considerably drained them off their resources. It is Old Acton however who has a claim on almost half of Cunningham's estate."

"If the villain is a local thief, then it shouldn't be a problem catching him," Holmes yawned.

The butler announced Inspector Forrester and the smart, young man stepped into the room. "Good morning, Colonel," he said. "I hope I'm not intruding, but we received word that Mr. Sherlock Holmes is here."

The Colonel waved his hand towards Holmes and the Inspector bowed. "We were wondering if you'd like to help us, Mr. Holmes," he said.

"Of course," Holmes replied, laughing. "We were talking about the case when you came in, Inspector. Maybe you can brief us about the details better."

"We had no clue in the Acton case," the Inspector confessed. "But we have plenty here to move ahead. There is no doubt that this was the same party. The man was also spotted."

"Ah!"

"Yes, sir. Mr. Cunningham saw him from the bedroom window as he ran away after murdering poor William Kirwan. Mr. Alec Cunningham spotted him from the back passage. It was quarter to twelve and Mr. Cunningham had just retired to bed. Mr. Alec was smoking a pipe in his room and both the men heard William's cries for help. Mr. Alec ran downstairs to investigate the matter. The back door was ajar and he reached the foot of the stairs to see two men wrestling outside. One of them fired a shot suddenly and the other man went down. The killer ran across the garden and over the hedge. Mr. Cunningham, while looking out of his bedroom window, saw the running man, but lost sight of him instantly. Mr. Alec attended to the wounded man and the killer escaped easily. He was a middle-sized man dressed in dark clothes. We are looking for him."

"What was William doing there? Did he say anything before his death?"

"Not a word. He lived at the lodge with his mother. It is likely that he walked towards the house to check if everything was all right. Everyone is on their guard here after the Acton robbery happened."

"Did William say anything to his mother before he left?"

"She's old and deaf and it's impossible to get any information out of her. Besides, she's also in deep shock. But there is one important clue! Take a look at this!"

The Inspector withdrew a small piece of torn paper from his notebook. "We found this between the thumb and finger of the dead man. It seems to be a fragment torn from a larger sheet. Observe that the time mentioned on it is the same as the hour in which the poor fellow met with his death. The murderer might have snatched the sheet from William or he might

'at quarter
to twelve learn
what maybe.'

have taken the fragment from the killer. It looks like an appointment."

Holmes studied the scrap of paper, which said,

'at quarter to twelve
learn what
maybe.'

"This is very interesting indeed," Holmes remarked, as he studied the paper with intense concentration. He buried his head in his hands and was silent for a few minutes, engrossed in deep thought. I was surprised to see his eyes shining brightly when he raised his face again. Holmes jumped to his feet. "I'd like to investigate this case as something in it is extremely fascinating. Colonel, if you will excuse me I shall leave you and Watson and accompany the Inspector. I shall return in half an hour."

Holmes returned with the Inspector only after one and a half hours. "Let us leave for Cunningham's house," he instructed. "There is something I must check. The matter becomes more and more interesting. We have seen interesting things. Firstly, we saw the dead body and then, we interviewed Mr. Cunningham and his son."

"What have you found out?"

"I am convinced that the crime is a strange one, indeed. The piece of paper in the dead man's hand is of vital importance. The clue that it gives is that the person who wrote that note was the same man who persuaded William to come there at that hour. But where is the rest of the sheet of paper?"

"I couldn't find it anywhere," the Inspector confessed.

"Why was it torn out of the dead man's hand? Why was the man so keen on possessing it? What has he done with it? It's likely that he pocketed it, without realizing that a corner remained in the dead man's hand. Getting the rest of the sheet would definitely help us solve this mystery."

"But how do we get the sheet without getting the murderer?"

"We'll think of a way. But how did the note arrive? By post? Or did someone get it personally?" Holmes asked.

"William received the letter by the afternoon post yesterday," the Inspector informed Holmes. "But he destroyed the envelope."

"Well done!" Holmes slapped the Inspector on the back. We had reached the lodge. "Colonel, I shall show you the scene of the crime now," Holmes stated. We saw a constable stationed at the kitchen door. Holmes ordered for the door to be opened. "Young Mr. Cunningham was on those very stairs when he saw those two men wrestling just where we are positioned now. Old Mr. Cunningham was at that window — the second on the left — and he spotted the murderer get away to the left of that bush. Then, Mr. Alec rushed out and knelt beside the wounded man. There are no marks to guide us as the ground is very hard."

We were joined by the two Cunninghams. "I'd like to clarify one point which I feel very strongly about," Holmes declared.

"What is that?" Mr. Cunningham asked.

"I think William came to the house after the burglar had arrived here, and not before. According to you, the door was forced but the burglar never got in."

"That's obvious," Mr. Cunningham said seriously. "Alec was still awake and he would have certainly heard someone moving about the house."

"Where were you?" Holmes asked Alec.

"I was smoking in my room."

"Your lamp was lit?"

"Yes."

"I find it strange that a burglar would choose to enter a house where the lights are still on," Holmes stated smilingly.

"Well, if the case was not so strange, Mr. Holmes, you wouldn't have been consulted," Alec replied. "But tell me, if the robber had arrived before Williams, wouldn't something be missing from the house?"

"It depends what the missing things are. Remember that he is a rather strange fellow. Think about all those things he chose to take from Acton's."

"Mr. Holmes, anything that you and the Inspector suggest will most certainly be done," Old Mr. Cunningham stated.

"I'd like you to offer a reward in the first place," Holmes instructed. "Sign this document that I have prepared. Fifty pounds should be enough I think."

"I would have happily given five hundred," Mr. Cunningham confessed and took the piece

of paper and pencil from Holmes. "But this is incorrect," Mr. Cunningham said as he read it.

"I wrote it in a hurry," Holmes confessed.

"You have written 'quarter to one on Tuesday morning...' instead of quarter to twelve," Mr. Cunningham said. I was pained at this revelation as Holmes was never imperfect. Holmes was obviously embarrassed as the Inspector raised his eyebrows and young Alec laughed mockingly. Mr. Cunningham corrected the error and handed the paper back to Holmes, who pocketed it.

Holmes expressed his wish to examine the house to determine if the burglar had stolen anything. We saw the marks on the door that had been pushed in.

"Don't you use bars?" Holmes enquired.

"We've never had the need to,"

"Don't you keep a dog?"

"We do. But he's chained to the other side of the house."

"When do the servants go to bed?

"At ten"

"It's strange that William was up so late that night," Holmes declared, and requested Mr. Cunningham to show us around the house. Holmes walked slowly, taking in each area very carefully.

"This is surely unnecessary, my good sir," Mr. Cunningham said impatiently. "That's my room at the end of the stairs and my son's room is beyond it. We would have surely known if the thief had come up here."

"But you must show me around a bit," Holmes insisted, and pushed open Alec's room. "Where does this window look out to?" he asked, as he entered the room and looked around.

"I hope you are satisfied now," asked Mr. Cunningham, sharply.

"Yes, thank you."

"Then, can we proceed to my room?"

"Yes, please."

But Holmes did something strange as the others left the room, and as he and I were the last to be leaving. To my astonishment, he deliberately knocked over the dish of oranges and the jug of water that rested near the foot of the bed. The glass broke into a hundred fragments and the oranges rolled in every corner of the room.

"Now, look what you've done, Watson! You've dirtied the carpet," he declared calmly. I started gathering the fruit from the floor in confusion. I clearly understood that this was part of Holmes's plan. But I had no idea what he was up to. The others followed my example as Holmes disappeared suddenly.

"Where has he gone now?" the Inspector exclaimed.

"The fellow is quite mad, in my opinion," Alec Cunningham declared, asking us to wait while he went and looked for Holmes with his father. The Cunninghams ran out of the room, leaving me, the Colonel and the Inspector staring at each other in confusion.

'Help! Help! Murder!' I recognized Holmes's voice instantly and I ran wildly from the room to the landing. The cries emerged from the room that we had visited earlier. We rushed inside to see the two Cunninghams bend over Holmes. The young one was clutching at his throat with both hands while the elder twisted his wrists. In an instant, the three of us had overpowered the Cunninghams and freed Holmes.

"Arrest them, Inspector," an exhausted Holmes ordered, gasping for breath.

"On what charge?"

"For the ruthless murder of their coachman, William Kirwan."

The expressions of fear and guilt on the faces of the Cunninghams were enough for the Inspector to arrest them instantly.

"What I really wanted was this," Holmes declared, waving a small, crumpled piece of paper.

"That's the remainder of the sheet!" the Inspector exclaimed. "Where was it?"

"Where I'd thought it would be," Holmes stated. "Please summon Mr. Acton. I shall explain everything after he arrives."

Holmes began his story after Mr. Acton arrived. "If young Cunningham's story was correct, and if the burglar had fled instantly after shooting William, he couldn't have possibly torn the paper from the hands of the dead man. The only man to do so then, could have been Alec Cunningham himself, as he was the only person near the scene of the crime. Having examined the piece of paper carefully, I noticed one strange thing in it. It has been written by two persons doing alternate words. See how strong the t's are of 'at' and 'to' and compare them with the weaker ones in the case

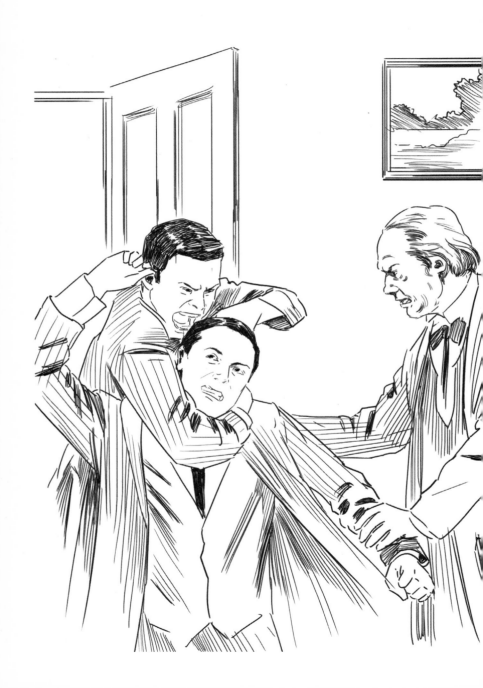

of 'quarter' and 'twelve' and you will recognize this abnormality easily.

"But why?"

"To conceal the identity of the writer," Holmes exclaimed.

"Brilliant!" Mr. Acton marveled.

"Now, let us come to an important point," Holmes continued. "The common thing between the two writers is that they are blood relatives. I'm convinced that a family mannerism can be traced by studying these two handwritings. After that, I visited the house with the Inspector to see what I had to. The wound on the dead man was inflicted by a revolver that had been fired from a distance of about four yards. No powder blackening of clothes was visible which should have been the case if two men had been wrestling with each other and if one had been shot at such close range. So, obviously Alec Cunningham had lied.

"But then, what was the motive of this strange crime? I decided to solve the reason for

the first burglary at Acton's to determine this. I learnt from the Colonel that some sort of lawsuit existed between the two parties and I was convinced that the Cunninghams had broken into Mr. Acton's house to steal an important document that would help their cause."

"Precisely," Mr. Acton said. "I have the claim upon half of their present estate and they would have won the case if they had got their hands on a single document. Thankfully, they were all with my lawyers."

"When they failed," Holmes continued smilingly, "they took off with some ordinary items to make it appear that it was a normal burglary. But what I wanted the most was to get my hands on the missing piece of the note. I was positive that Alec had torn it from the dead man's hand. I was almost sure that he had shoved it into the pocket of his dressing gown as there was nowhere else he could have put it then. But was it still there? One could

only find out. First, I made Old Cunningham write 'twelve' on the reward document by pretending I had made a mistake so that I could compare his handwriting with that upon the paper."

"Oh, what a fool I've been," I exclaimed.

"I could sense your disappointment on seeing my weakness, Watson," Holmes laughed. "I made them busy by upsetting the table and rushed off to investigate if the missing piece of paper was still in Alec's dressing gown. I had hardly got the paper when the two Cunninghams were upon me."

Cunningham confessed everything when he saw that the case against him was so strong. Apparently, William had secretly followed his two masters when they raided Mr. Acton's house. William started blackmailing his masters when he had them in his power. But Alec was a dangerous man to play games with and so, they decided to kill William.

If you will only come around at quarter to twelve to the east gate you will learn what will surprise you and be of the greatest service to you and Annie Morrison. But say nothing to anyone upon the matter.

"What about the note, Holmes?" I asked, when everything was clear.

Sherlock Holmes spread out the entire paper before all of us.

'If you will only come around at quarter to twelve to the east gate you will learn what will surprise you and be of the greatest service to you and Annie Morrison. But say nothing to anyone upon the matter.'

"I expected exactly what was written on the note," Holmes stated with satisfaction. Of course, the relation between Alec Cunningham, William Kirwan and Annie Morrison is not known, the trap however was cleverly baited. It was also the traces in the heredity shown in the handwriting that helped us solve the case."

Chapter Five

The Stockbroker's Clerk

Last June, I accompanied Sherlock Holmes for a case in Birmingham as I had some work there.

"What is the case, Holmes?" I asked.

"I'll tell you all about it in the train, Watson. My client is waiting in a cab outside. Can you come at once?"

We boarded the four wheeler to go to the station. A strongly built, young man with an honest face and a thin, yellow moustache sat inside. He wore a neat black suit and a shiny top hat. His round face reflected happiness but his eyes were troubled. But I only came to know about his story when we were on the train to Birmingham.

"Mr. Pycroft, please narrate your interesting story again," Holmes requested the man. "My friend Dr. Watson is interested to hear it and his opinion might be helpful."

"The worst part of this story," the man turned to me with a twinkle in his eyes and said, "is that it makes me look like a fool."

"I used to be employed at Coxon and Woodhouse's, of Draper's Gardens. It was the company's repayment of the Venezuelan loan that had put an end to my five year long service to them. They were paying me three pounds a week there and even though I tried hard to get a job elsewhere, I was unsuccessful. My hopes rose when I spotted a vacancy in Mawson & Williams's, the richest house in London. It is a reputed stock-broking firm in Lombard Street. The advertisement was to be replied to by letter only. I put in my application and received a reply that I could begin my new duties from next Monday. My salary would be four pounds

a week and the job responsibilities would be the same as at Coxon's. Now comes the weird part of the entire business. I was residing at Hampstead, 17 Potter's Terrace. The very evening that I had received my appointment letter, I received a visit from a man named Arthur Pinner. He claimed to be a Financial Agent and was a middle-sized, dark-haired, dark-eyed, black-bearded man. He spoke rather sharply.

" 'Mr. Hall Pycroft, I presume?'

" 'Yes, sir,' I replied, offering him a chair.

" 'Lately working with Coxon & Woodhouse's and currently engaged with Mawson's?'

" 'That's right.'

" 'Well, the truth is that news of your financial capabilities has reached me. Parker, a former Coxon's manager, used to keep praising you.'

" 'Naturally, I was very pleased to hear this as it was unimaginable for me that I would be complimented in the City.'

" 'Have you been connected with the market when you were jobless?' he enquired.

" 'Yes, sir. I make sure to read the stock exchange list every morning.'

" 'That is impressive and displays real application,' he exclaimed. 'That is the way to grow. You deserve much more than a clerkship at Mawson's!'

I was stunned at this statement. "'Well sir,' I replied modestly. 'Others do not think of me as highly as you do, and the truth is that I had a tough time getting a job. Hence, I am very happy with it.'

" 'Ha, man; You should rise above it. My offer is gigantic when compared to Mawson's. My offer to you is that of Business Manager at the Franco-Midland Hardware Company Limited, with a hundred thirty four branches in the towns and villages of France.'

"I almost stopped breathing. 'I've never heard of it,' was what I could manage to say.

" 'That's understandable as everything has been kept very quiet. The capital has totally been privately subscribed, you see. My brother, Harry Pinner, is the Managing Director and asked me to source a young man who specializes in Stock. Parker recommended you highly, and that's what brought me here. We offer you five hundred to begin with!'

" 'Five hundred a year!!' I exclaimed in great surprise and happiness.

" 'That is just to begin with, of course. You'll get a raise later.'

I was shaking in my chair in excitement. But then, the faint shadow of doubt crept in my mind. "'I must be frank with you, sir,' I stated. 'Now, although Mawson's offer is only two hundred a year, it is a safer company. I know so less about your organization that it is really…'

" 'A smart man, indeed,' he exclaimed. 'Mere talk won't suffice, and that's absolutely right. Now, here's a hundred pound note as

an advance against your salary,' he stated and handed over the note to me.

" 'That is very generous,' I replied. 'When do I have to assume my new duties?'

The man instructed me to be in Birmingham at one the following day.

" 'Take this note,' he said. 'It will take you to my brother who sits at 126b Corporation Street. The temporary offices of the company are located there.'

" 'Thank you, Mr. Pinner,' I replied.

" 'There are some formalities that need completion,' he said. 'Please write down on this piece of paper. "I am perfectly willing to act as the Business Manager of Franco-Midland Hardware Company Limited, at a minimum salary of 500 pounds."'

"I did as instructed, and he pocketed the paper. 'And what will you do about Mawson's?' he asked.

" 'I shall write and resign,' I replied.

" 'No, I don't want you to do that. I had an argument over you with Mawson's manager. I had visited him to enquire about you and he was angry about it. He accused me of poaching you away from the firm's services. After a long time, I lost my temper as well. "You should pay good men a good price if you want to employ their services." I had declared.

" 'He would rather choose our small offer than your big one,' he had replied.

" ' " You'll never hear from him after I've made my offer to him," I had stated.

" ' "We'll see. We have picked him up from the gutter and he won't abandon us so easily." Those were his exact words.'

" 'How dare he say such a thing!' I cried. 'I've never ever seen him in my life. I shall certainly follow your advice and not write to him.'

" 'Very good!' the man said, as he rose from his chair. 'I'm delighted that I have managed to source such a good man for my

brother. Remember to meet your one o' clock appointment tomorrow. Goodnight!'

"The very next day, I was off to Birmingham in a train. After keeping my things in a hotel at New Street, I reached the address that had been provided to me. I was fifteen minutes early for the appointment. 126b was a small passage between two large shops. This led to a stone stair, which led to many flats that were rented out as offices to professionals and companies. The names of the occupants were painted at the bottom of the wall. But the name of Franco-Midland Hardware Company Limited was nowhere to be seen. I stood there, wondering if the entire thing had been a hoax, when a man approached me. He looked very similar to the man who had visited me the night before, except for the fact that he was clean shaven and his hair was lighter.

" 'Are you Mr. Hall Pycroft?' he enquired. I realized that apart from the figure, the voice matched the other man's voice as well.

" 'Yes,' I replied.

" 'I was expecting you as my brother's note reached me today morning,' he explained.

" 'I was looking for the offices.'

" 'We don't have our name up yet, as we moved into these temporary offices just last week. Come this way, please.'

We moved up the stairs and entered a couple of empty, dusty little rooms. My vision of a big office with shiny tables and rows of clerks, that I was accustomed to, came crashing down. All that was present were two chairs and a small table. The rooms were dusty and uncarpeted.

" 'Don't be disappointed, Mr. Pycroft,' my new employer said reassuringly, 'We haven't brought in any furniture yet. Please take a seat and let me have your letter.'

" 'You have made a good impression on my brother, Arthur,' he said after he read the letter. 'I trust him totally and we are happy to have you join us.'

" 'What will my duties be?,' I enquired.

" 'In time, you will manage the business of the company in Paris, dealing with English crockery items. The purchase will take a week to complete, and in the meantime, you will work in Birmingham. This is a directory of Paris,' he said, taking out a big, red book from a drawer. 'It has the names of the traders. Take it home with you and mark off all the hardware sellers, along with their addresses. I need the lists on Monday by noon. Have a good day, Mr. Pycroft.'

"I returned to the hotel with the big book tucked under my arm and with my heart full of doubt. The shabby offices and the entire episode had left a sour impression on my mind. But as I lacked money, I concentrated on the task at hand. I got as far as H by Monday and visited my boss, who told me to keep working at it till Wednesday and then return. But I finished the job only on Friday, and visited Mr. Harry Pinner with it.

" 'Thank you,' he said. 'Now, make a list of all the furniture shops selling crockery. You should come and let me know how you are getting on by seven tomorrow evening. But make sure that you don't over exert yourself,' he said, and laughed, and I could spot his second tooth on the left hand side. It was badly stuffed with gold!"

Holmes rubbed his hands delightedly while I stared in amazement at our client. "You might appear surprised, Dr. Watson," he said. "But this is exactly what happened. "When I spoke to the other man in London, I happened to notice that his tooth was stuffed in a similar fashion. The glint of the gold caught my attention in both cases. I am positive that it is the same man with the voice and the figure matching as well. Agreed that the two are brothers, but it is too much of a coincidence that the same tooth is stuffed in an identical manner. I was totally confused when I exited his office. Why had

he sent me to Birmingham all the way from London? What was the reason for writing a letter to himself? I could not make sense of it. Then, I remembered Mr. Sherlock Holmes."

Holmes addressed me now, "Watson, I think we should interview Mr. Arthur Harry Pinner in his temporary offices of the Franco-Midland Hardware Company Limited."

"But how?" I asked.

"That's easy," Hall Pycroft said cheerfully. "You can pose as friends of mine who are looking for jobs."

"Let's take a look at this gentleman, then," Holmes declared. At about seven in the evening, we approached the offices of Mr. Pinner.

"There is no point reaching early," our client stated. "It seems that he only visits the place to see me. The place remains empty till the hour he names to meet me."

"That's very suggestive, indeed," Holmes commented.

At seven that evening, we reached the Corporation street where the company's offices were located.

"There he is!" Pycroft exclaimed. "He's walking ahead of us, right there."

We saw a small, dark, smartly dressed man walking on the other side of the road, with a newspaper tucked under his arm. We followed Pycroft as he led the way to climb five stories and entered a bare room that was unfurnished. The man we had seen on the street sat at the single table with his evening newspaper spread out before him. As we entered, he cast us a look of great sadness and terror. His eyes were wild and he was sweating.

"You look sick, Mr. Pinner," Pycroft exclaimed. The man licked his dry lips before he replied, "Yes, I'm unwell. But who are these two gentlemen with you?"

"Mr. Harris of Bermondsey and Mr. Price from this town," the clerk replied. "They are

friends of mine and are hopeful of finding employment with your company."

"Yes, Yes!" Mr. Pinner cried. "We shall be able to do something for you. But now, please leave me alone. I beg you to leave, for God's sake!"

Holmes and I stared at each other, but Pycroft approached the man. "But Mr. Pinner, you are forgetting that you had called me here to take further directions from you," he reminded him.

"Of course, Mr. Pycroft, please wait here for a moment. I shall be back in about three minutes." Mr. Pinner rose and walked out through a door at a far corner of the room, closing the door behind him.

"Is he running away?" Holmes asked.

"Not possible," Pycroft replied. "That door leads into an inner room."

"There is no exit?"

"No."

A sharp knocking noise emerged from the inner door just then.

"Why is the man knocking on his own door?" Pycroft exclaimed.

The rat-tat-tat noise became louder and was followed by a low gushing, gargling noise. Holmes excitedly ran forward, pushed against the door and barged into the room, followed by us. A coat was lying on the floor and from a hook behind the door, with the aid of the elastic straps of his own pants, hung the honorable Managing Director of Franco-Midland Hardware Company Limited. I held him up by catching him round the waist instantly while Holmes and Pycroft untied the elastic bands. We carried him to the other room after that, where he lay with a grey face and purple lips.

"What do you think, Watson?" Holmes asked as I examined the man. The pulse was faint, but I detected that the breathing was becoming stronger. There was also a shivering of the eyelids.

"He will live now," I stated and poured some cold water on the man's face. "But he could have died."

"We should call the police now," Holmes commented. "But I'd like to give them a complete case when they arrive."

"It's all a strange mystery to me," Pycroft exclaimed but Holmes signaled for silence.

"It's all perfectly clear," Holmes stated. "It is this last move."

"You comprehend the rest then?"

"Yes, don't you see how suggestive it is that he made you write a declaration?"

"No," Pycroft admitted.

"My dear young friend, all they wanted was a specimen of your handwriting."

"Why?"

"Simply because someone wanted to imitate your handwriting to serve their purpose. But now, let's examine the second point. Why did Pinner insist that you do not resign from

your position? The fact is, that the manager of this prestigious institution where you were supposed to join has never seen you. So, he wouldn't suspect a thing if someone else going by the name of Mr. Hall Pycroft walks in to join the company on Monday morning."

"Oh Lord, I've been so blind," Pycroft exclaimed.

"Someone with a different handwriting than yours would most certainly have been caught," Holmes explained further. "But it was imperative that you do not come into contact with anyone at Mawson's. So, in order to keep you engaged, they employed you with a false company, so that you could not go to London.

"But why pretend to be your own brother?"

"That's easy. There are only two men in this game. One is impersonating you at the office while the other is pretending to be your manager. It would have been suspicious if your boss came to hire you himself. Hence the disguise. You might not have recognized the man if not for the gold stuffing."

"What shall we do, Mr. Holmes?" Pycroft asked desperately.

"We need to wire Mawson's to find out if all is well. Then, we need to find out if anyone is working there using your name. But what is unclear is why this man tried to hang himself."

"The newspaper," a voice croaked behind us. The man was sitting up now. His eyes deathly pale and he rubbed his throat with his hands in a nervous manner.

"Of course!" Holmes exclaimed. "The paper! What an idiot I have been!"

Holmes flattened the newspaper on the table. "Look at this, Watson," he yelled.

"'Crime in the City! Murder at Mawson and Williams's. Attempted Robbery Foiled! Criminal Captured!

Here's what the news below it said,

'An attempted robbery has resulted in the death of one man and the capture of the criminal this afternoon in the City. Mawson & Williams, the reputed financial house have been the guardians of securities amounting over a million sterling. An armed watchman stands guard day and night in the building. A new clerk called Hall Pycroft was engaged by the firm last week. This person apparently was none other than Beddington, the notorious forger and robber, who had come out of jail with his brother recently.

Under the false name, using unknown methods, Beddington had obtained information regarding the inner security vaults. As its customary at Mawson's for the clerks to leave at noon on Saturdays, it was surprising for Sergeant Tuson of the City Police to spot a man with a carpet bag exit the building at twenty minutes past one.

He followed the man and arrested him with the assistance of Constable Pollock. Almost a hundred thousand pounds worth of American railway bonds were found in the bag. The

dead body of the unfortunate watchman was found stuffed in the largest safe on proper examination of the office. Beddington had entered the building by pretending that he had left something behind. Then, he had killed the watchman and robbed the firm. His brother, who normally works with him, has not participated in this job as far as we know. But the police are trying to locate him.'

"Well, Watson, we can surely save the police some trouble when it comes to that," Holmes stated, as he cast a look at the tired figure huddled up by the window.

Chapter Six

The Yellow Face

It was a day in early spring when a tall muscular man paid a visit to Sherlock Holmes at Baker Street. He was about forty years of age and was dressed in a smart, dark grey suit. He moved his hand over his forehead in a nervous manner after he was seated.

"How can I help you?" Holmes asked.

"I need your advice, sir. My whole life appears to be ruined. I don't know what to do."

The man spoke in short, jerky bursts, as if it was causing him immense pain to recollect the events that had brought him to Holmes.

"It is not proper for one to talk about one's private life with strangers," the man stated. "But I'm very upset and I must have your advice."

"Mr. Grant Munro..." Holmes began, and the man jumped up from his chair in astonishment. "What? You know my name?"

"Well, I happened to spot your name written upon the lining of your hat," Holmes explained. "We shall try our best to help you. Please tell us the details of your case."

"Mr. Holmes, I have been married for three years now," the man began. "My wife and I have had a happy marriage and we love each other. We haven't had a single difference in thought, word or action. But since last Monday, I'm troubled as there is something in her life that I'm unaware of. That separates the two of us somewhat and I want to find out the reason behind it."

"Go on, Mr. Munro," Holmes said.

"Effie was a young widow of twenty-five when I met her first. She was Mrs. Hebron

then. In her younger days, she married a lawyer called Hebron when she went to Atlanta, America. They had a child but the yellow fever outbreak killed both the husband and child. I have seen his death certificate. She returned to Pinner then to live with her aunt. Her husband had left her about four thousand and five hundred pounds. I met her six months later. The two of us fell in love and decided to get married. I am a hop merchant by profession and make approximately seven or eight hundred. We are well off and reside in a villa at Norbury. It is a small countryside with just one inn and two houses above us. There is a small cottage with a large field next door. I am away to the City on business mostly. When we married, my wife gave me all her property, much against my wishes. But she was absolutely insistent about it and I didn't want to upset her. Just six weeks ago, she asked me for a hundred pounds. I was a little surprised as it was a large amount. So, I asked her why she needed it.

" 'Oh, Jack,' she said playfully. 'Please give it to me.'

" 'Of course I will. But first tell me why you need it.'

" 'Someday, maybe Jack, but not now.'

"This was the first time a secret existed between us. But I gave her a cheque and forgot about the entire episode. The cottage next door had been vacant for eight months. So, I was naturally surprised to see a pile of carpets and other things lying on the porch. It was obvious that someone had come to live there. As I walked past the cottage, I saw someone watching me from one of the upper windows. I couldn't see the face clearly as I was a fair distance away, but there was something unnatural and inhuman about that yellow face.

"My curiosity pushed me to have a closer look. So, I moved forward, but the face suddenly disappeared. I stood there for five minutes, trying to analyze the features but I couldn't determine if it was the face of a man or a woman. It wasn't exactly yellow but was almost chalky white in color. It was shockingly unearthly. It disturbed me to such an extent that I decided to discover who our new neighbour was. I knocked at the door and a tall, gaunt woman with a harsh face answered it. I introduced myself and offered my help in case she needed it.

" 'Yes. We'll ask you when we want you,' she said, in a strong Northern accent and slammed the door shut on my face. I was irritated and returned home. I did not disclose the incident to my wife as I didn't want to upset her. However, I did mention to her before I fell asleep that the cottage next door was now occupied. I did not receive a response from her. Despite being a sound sleeper, I couldn't sleep a wink that night. I had a strange premonition that something was going on.

"I half-opened my eyes to see my wife putting on her coat and then, her slippers. I was about to ask her where she was going but changed my mind when I saw her face. It was deathly pale and she was breathing rapidly. She was looking at me from time to time to check if I was awake. Confident that I was asleep, she moved noiselessly from the room. I heard the front door open. It was three in the morning! What on earth was my wife doing outside at this time? I sat in bed puzzled, trying to figure out a logical explanation for my wife's behavior. After twenty minutes, I heard the door open and my wife coming up the stairs.

" 'Where have you been, Effie?' I asked as she entered. Startled to see me awake at that hour of the night, she gave a grasping cry. My wife, who had always been frank and honest, was now hiding something from me. And when she spoke next, I could sense guilt in her voice.

" 'You're awake, Jack!' she laughed nervously.

" 'Where have you been?' I asked sternly.

" 'I understand your surprise,' she said with trembling fingers. 'But I felt as if I was choking. I needed some fresh air. I feel much better now.'

"Not once did she look at me when she said this. Her voice did not seem natural and I knew that she was lying. But I said nothing, even though I was very suspicious and hurt. What was my wife hiding from me? Where had she been? I could not sleep that night! The next day, I could not go to the City as I was too disturbed to concentrate on work. My wife and I did not exchange a single word during breakfast and I left to take a walk after that. I returned by one o' clock and as I passed the cottage, I stopped to look at the windows. Imagine my surprise when I saw my wife walk out suddenly. I was frozen but my wife seemed more affected to see me. She just stood at the door with a white face and wide open eyes.

" 'Oh, Jack,' she said. 'I've just been inside to see if I could help our new neighbours.'

" 'So, this is where you came last night.'

" 'What do you mean?' she exclaimed.

" 'I am positive you came here. Who are these people that you should visit them at such an hour?' I demanded angrily.

" 'I haven't been here before, Jack,'

" 'You are a liar. I shall find out the truth myself by entering the cottage.'

" 'No, Jack!' she gasped, and grabbed me by the sleeve to pull me back with all her might as I tried to enter the cottage. 'Don't do this, Jack. I swear I'll tell you everything someday,' she promised. I tried to shake her off but she pulled me harder.

" 'Trust me, Jack. Trust me just once and you shall never regret it. You know that I would never keep a secret from you if it was not for your own good. Our whole lives are at stake, Jack. If you come away with me now, all will be well. But if you force your way into that cottage, everything will be over between us.'

"Mr. Holmes, she was in such a state that I stood shell-shocked before the door."

" 'I will trust you on one condition,' I finally said. 'You are never to enter this cottage again without my permission.'

"My wife agreed to this condition with a huge sigh of relief and led me away from the cottage still pulling at my sleeve. I glanced backwards to see the yellow face watching us from the upper window. What was the link that existed between my wife and that strange creature? It was a strange puzzle and I knew my mind would not know peace till I solved it.

"I stayed at home for two days after that and my wife kept her word. But she broke her promise on the third day. I went to town that day, but returned earlier than usual. I learnt from the startled maid that my wife had gone out for a walk and I was instantly suspicious. As I went upstairs, I saw the maid run towards the cottage from my window. Then, it was all clear.

My wife had gone to the cottage and instructed the maid to call her as soon as I had returned. Enraged, I rushed downstairs to make my way towards the cottage. I was hell-bent to end the matter once and for all.

"I spotted my wife and the maid rushing back along the lane but did not stop to talk to them. I did not even knock after I reached the cottage door. I just turned the handle and entered the passage. Everything was still and silent! There was no sign of the woman who had answered the door the previous day. I rushed into all the rooms but they were all empty. I entered the room from where that strange face had stared at me. But it was empty as well! It was a warm and elegant room but what I saw on the fireplace angered me greatly. It was a photograph of my wife!

"I left the cottage with great sorrow in my heart and entered my house. I was too hurt and angry to speak to my wife as she met me in the hall.

" 'I'm sorry I broke my promise, Jack,' she said. 'But if you knew everything, you would forgive me.'

" 'Tell me everything, then,' I demanded.

" 'I can't, Jack,' she pleaded. I refused to speak to her unless she did and left the house. This happened yesterday and I haven't seen her since then, Mr. Holmes. It suddenly struck me today morning that you were the best person to seek advice from, and so, I rushed here.'

Holmes sat in silence for some time. "Have you ever seen the photograph of her late husband?" he finally asked.

"No! All her papers were destroyed in a great fire in Atlanta which happened, shortly after her husband's death."

"But you did mention that she had a death certificate."

"Yes, she had a duplicate of that."

"Did you come across anyone who knew her in America?"

"No."

"Did she ever talk about going back to Atlanta?"

"No."

"I think the people in the cottage vacated it once they knew you were coming. They must have returned by now. I'd advise you to return to Norbury at once. If you feel that they have returned, do not force your way in again. Telegram us instead, and we shall be there in an hour's time after receipt of your telegram," Holmes instructed.

"What if it is empty?"

"Then we shall arrive tomorrow morning," Holmes replied. Holmes asked me what I felt about the case after our client left.

"I think the woman's first husband is in that cottage," I stated.

"What makes you assume so?"

"The woman was married in America and abandoned her husband after he caught some

ugly disease. She returned home and started life afresh. Suddenly, her first husband and that rough woman find out her whereabouts and start blackmailing her. She pays them a hundred pounds but they want more. That's what I think. But we are helpless till we receive that telegram."

The telegram arrived that evening.

"The cottage is still occupied. Will meet you at the station at seven o'clock, and take no steps until then." it said.

We met Mr. Grant Munro at the station and he told us that he planned to force his way again into the cottage, with us as his witnesses this time. It was a very dark night and Mr. Munro guided us towards the cottage. But just as we were about to enter, a woman stepped out of the shadows and stood before us.

"Don't do it Jack!" she pleaded. "I knew you'd return today. But please trust me and you'll never regret it."

"I have trusted you far too long, Effie," he replied, pushing her to one side. Then, we rushed up the stairs to the upper room. A little girl sat in a corner, with her face turned away from us. She had long white gloves on and was wearing a red frock. I cried in surprise and terror as she turned towards us. Her face was totally white! But the mystery was revealed instantly. With a laugh, Holmes stepped forward, moved his hand behind the child's ear, and peeled off the mask she was wearing. A small, coal black negress stood before us, laughing with bright, white teeth.

"What is the meaning of this?" demanded Grant Munro, angrily.

"Let me explain," the lady shouted, running into the room. "Although my husband died at Atlanta, my child survived."

"Your child?" Munro stated. She pointed to a large silver locket in her neck. "You have never seen this open."

"I didn't know it opened."

She opened it to reveal the picture of a handsome African man. "John Hebron, of Atlanta," she revealed. "He was a true gentleman, and I abandoned my family to marry him. Not once did I regret my decision as long as he was alive. It is my luck that our child took after his people and not mine. Little Lucy might be darker than her own father. But dark or fair, she is my own baby!"

Little Lucy ran across the room and hugged her mother. "I left her in America only because of her weak health and our devoted servant looked after her. I have never imagined abandoning my only child. But when I met you, Jack and fell in love with you, I was scared to tell you about Lucy. I was afraid to lose you and didn't have the courage to tell you. I have kept this secret from you for three years but I longed to see my child.

"So I took a hundred pounds from you and sent it to the nurse, with instructions about this cottage so they could come as our neighbours. I took all the precautions; I kept the child indoors and even covered her up so that they'd be no gossip about a black child in the neighbourhood if she was spotted at the window.

"Jack, you were the one who first told me about the cottage being occupied. I was so excited I couldn't sleep. I rushed there without even waiting for morning. But you spotted me and my troubles began. Now, Jack, please tell me what is our fate? What will happen to my child and me?" she clasped her hands and awaited her husband's reply.

Grant Munro broke his silence after ten minutes. But his reply was that of love! He lifted little Lucy and kissed her. Still holding her, he extended the other hand towards his wife as he turned towards the door. "I think we can talk about this more comfortably at home, Effie," he

stated. "I might not be a very good man, Effie, but I think I'm a better man than you have given me credit for."

Holmes pulled at my sleeves. "I feel, Watson," he said with a wink, "that we shall be more useful in London now than in Norbury."

Chapter Seven

Silver Blaze

The Wessex Cup was the talk of the City. The favourite champion horse had mysteriously disappeared all of a sudden, just one week before the event and his trainer had been brutally murdered.

Just two days after this incident, Sherlock Holmes and I were headed by train to Dartmoor, where this had happened. "You've read about the murder of John Straker and Silver Blaze going missing, haven't you Watson?"

"I have read the newspapers," I replied.

"Let me give you my account," Holmes stated and began, "Silver Blaze is now in his

fifth year and has won a lot of prizes. He was the clear favourite for the Wessex Cup, but there are many rivals who do not want Silver Blaze to win next Tuesday. So, the horse was guarded carefully at King's Pyland, where the Colonel's training stable was located. The trainer, John Straker, has been with the Colonel for five years as a jockey and seven years as a trainer. He has always been a faithful servant. Three lads reported to him and one of them sat up each night in the stable while the others slept in the loft. All three lads were devoted servants. Straker was a married man and he lived in a small villa located a couple of hundred yards from the stables. He has no children, has one maidservant and is well-off.

Dartmoor is a secluded place but there are a couple of small villas to the North. Just two miles away, exists the larger training establishment of Mapleton. This belongs to Lord Backwater and is managed by Silas Brown. Other than this,

the moor is complete wilderness. Last Monday evening, the stables were locked up at nine o' clock. Two of the lads went to the trainer's house, where they had supper in the kitchen while the third lad, Ned Hunter remained on guard. The maid, Edith Baxter, carried down a meal for him at nine-thirty. It was a flavoured mutton curry. The maid carried a lantern as it was very dark. She had almost reached the stables when a man suddenly emerged from the darkness and called out to her to stop. He was about thirty years old, and was wearing a grey suit, a cloth cap and long shoes. He held a heavy stick with a lead handle and appeared nervous.

" 'I know that a stable boy sleeps alone at the stables every night,' he stated. 'Maybe you are carrying his supper to him. Take this and ensure that he has this tonight,' the man said as he took out a piece of white paper from the pocket of his waistcoat. 'I shall pay you well if you do so.'

"The girl was so scared that she ran off into the stables. She had just begun to tell Hunter what had transpired when the man peeped in through the window.

" 'Good evening,' he said, 'May I have a word with you?'

" 'Regarding what?' Hunter asked.

" 'Silver Blaze!'

" 'You're one of those touts, eh? I'll show you what we do to them at King's Pyland,' Hunter said, and ran to unloose the dog. The girl ran back to the house and saw the stranger leaning through the window. But he had disappeared a minute later, when Hunter had arrived with the dog. Hunter could not locate him.

"Did the stable boy leave the door unlocked behind him?" I asked suddenly.

"Excellent, Watson," Holmes complimented me. "I had thought of the possibility and had written to Dartmoor police yesterday about it. Apparently, the boy had locked the door

before leaving. Also, the window was not large enough for a man to enter the stables. Hunter sent a message to Straker informing him about what had happened and the trainer was uneasy. Mrs. Straker discovered him dressing at one in the morning. He said he was worried about the horses and would go to check on them. She pleaded with him not to go as it was raining. But he left after putting on his large coat.

"When Mrs Straker awoke at seven in the morning, she discovered that her husband had still not returned. She dressed speedily and left for the stables, accompanied by her maid. The door was open and Hunter was sleeping soundly inside. Silver Blaze had disappeared and there was no sign of his trainer! The two lads sleeping inside the loft were roused and they said they had heard nothing during the night. Hunter was apparently drugged and could not be woken up.

"Mrs. Straker rushed outside with the two lads to look for her husband. Their first thought was that the trainer had taken Silver Blaze out for a stroll. But they were shocked to find John Straker's overcoat hanging from a bush, almost a quarter of a mile from the stables. Just below the bush, lay the dead body of the poor trainer. His head had been smashed by a heavy weapon and he had received wounds on the thigh with some sharp instrument. He held a small blood clotted knife in his right hand and his left hand held a red and black silk tie. The maid confirmed that the stranger had worn this very tie.

"Regarding Silver Blaze, the impressions of the hooves were aplenty on the ground; but they stopped eventually. Later, a blood test revealed that Hunter's food had been drugged with opium. Well, Watson, these are the main facts about the case. Now, let me brief you about the progress made by the police.

"Inspector Gregory is in charge of the case and he has arrested a man named Fitzroy Simpson. This person bets on horses and is engaged in a bit of bookmaking business in the London sporting clubs. He had bet against the favourite, Silver Blaze, for as much as five thousand pounds.

"After being arrested, he said he had arrived at Dartmoor to obtain information about the horses at King's Pyland. He had also wanted to find out about Desborough, the second favourite horse in charge of Silas Brown at the Mapleton stables. He was insistent that he had neither murdered anyone nor stolen the horse. He just wanted to gather information. He said that he had lost his tie when asked about it. His stick, with a lead handle, could be the weapon that killed Straker. But there was not a single mark of violence on Simpson."

"Is it possible that Straker might have harmed himself with his own knife while he was struggling?" I enquired.

"It's possible," Holmes replied thoughtfully. We reached Dartmoor in the evening and were received by two gentlemen at the station — Colonel Ross, the famous sportsman and Inspector Gregory.

"Thank you for coming, Mr. Holmes," the Colonel stated. "The Inspector has done everything he could, but I want to find my horse."

Inspector Gregory explained the case in detail after we were seated in the carriage.

"The evidence against Fitzroy Simpson is strong. I am positive he is the thief," he stated. Holmes shook his head. "Why would he want to take the horse out of the stable? If he wished to injure the horse, he could have done it there itself. Did he possess a duplicate key? Where did he obtain the opium from? And most importantly, where can he hide the horse, being a stranger in these parts?"

"The opium was purchased most probably from London," the Inspector replied. "He must

have hidden the key after using it. The horse could be concealed at the bottom of one of the old mines or pits upon the moor."

"I believe that there is another training stable nearby?" Holmes enquired.

"Yes. Silas Brown, the trainer there, has placed large bets on the event himself. He was also a rival of Straker. But we did not find anything after examining their stables."

Our driver pulled up before a neat little red brick villa and we got down. Holmes wanted to see the things found in the dead man's pockets and the Inspector took us to the sitting room, where he displayed a small heap of items before us. There were two candles, a box of matches, a few papers and a knife with a rather delicate, inflexible blade.

"This is a very strange knife," Holmes commented as he examined it closely. "If I'm correct, it must have been found in the dead man's grasp. Do you use such a knife in medical science, Watson?"

"It is used for eye operations," I replied.

"I thought as much. A delicate instrument used for delicate work. It is a strange thing for a man to carry on a night like that."

"His wife said it was lying on the dressing table and he picked it up in a hurry as he left," the Inspector stated.

"What about these papers?"

"One is a letter of instructions from the Colonel. The second is a milliner's account for thirty-seven pounds fifteen addressed to a certain William Derbyshire. Mrs. Straker has informed us that Derbyshire was her late husband's friend and his letters were addressed here sometimes."

"Madam Derbyshire had expensive tastes," Holmes commented, after studying the paper. A woman with a thin and pale face entered the room just then. "Have you found them?" she gasped.

"Not yet, Mrs. Straker," the Inspector replied. "But Mr. Holmes here is helping us."

"Mrs. Straker, didn't I meet you at a garden party at Plymouth sometime back?" Holmes enquired.

"No, sir, you are mistaken," she replied.

"Oh! I thought you were the one. Weren't you wearing a flowing silver coloured dress?"

"Never."

Holmes apologized and followed the Inspector outside. We walked to the place where the body had been discovered.

"There was no wind that night, if I'm correct," Holmes asked.

"No. But there was heavy rain."

"So, the overcoat had not blown against that bush. Instead, it had been placed there."

"Perhaps," the Inspector replied. "I have in this bag one of Straker's boots that he wore that night, one of Fitzroy Simpson's shoes and a cast horseshoe of Silver Blaze."

Holmes first studied the trampled mud marks in front of him. Then, he brought out

the boots from the bag and compared the impressions of each one with the marks on the ground. Then, he proceeded to search the bushes. Colonel Ross looked at his watch and asked the Inspector to accompany him. "I need your advice on several matters."

The Inspector and the Colonel walked back together as Holmes and I took a slow walk across the moor.

"What if the horse had bolted away during or after the tragedy?" Holmes said to me. "Where would he have gone to? Horses are very instinctive creatures, Watson. Left alone, he could have either gone to King's Pyland or Mapleton. There's no way he'd be running wild upon the moor. If he had done so, he would have been spotted by now.

"But where is Silver Blaze then?" I demanded.

"As he is not at King's Pyland, he must surely be at Mapleton," Holmes stated. "This part of the moor leads there and from here one can see

the long hollow over yonder. It must have been very wet on Monday night as it was raining. If our theory is right, the horse must have crossed that stretch and left his tracks in the process. Let's look for them."

We spotted the horse's tracks as soon as we arrived at the hollow. The horseshoe in our possession matched the impression perfectly. Following the tracks, we crossed the hollow and then lost the tracks for about half a mile. But we picked them up again close to Mapleton. Holmes saw the tracks first and a man's tracks were visible next to Silver Blaze's tracks.

"The horse was not alone now!" I exclaimed.

"Precisely, my dear Watson!"

The tracks ended at the gates of the Mapleton stables and as we came nearer, the big, muscular man, Silas Brown blocked our path.

"What is your business here?" he growled.

"We wish to talk to you for ten minutes, good sir," Holmes replied.

"Off with you," he growled. "I have no time to talk with you. Go away now or I'll set a dog upon you."

Holmes bent forward and whispered something into the man's ears and he started violently. "All right, come in if you wish to," he offered. Holmes spoke to the man for twenty minutes instead of ten. But Silas Brown changed completely in that time. His face turned deathly pale and his hands shook nervously. "Your instructions will be followed, sir," he stated. "Make sure there is no mistake," Holmes warned the man.

"It shall be there, sir,"

We left Brown there and walked towards King's Pyland.

"He has the horse then?" I asked.

"Yes of course. He found it wandering near his stables."

"But the stables have been searched," I protested.

"Oh, it's just in another colour now," Holmes said coolly.

I was stunned but I could not ask him anything further as we were back at the trainer's house where the Colonel and the Inspector awaited us.

"Your horse will run on Tuesday, Colonel." Holmes declared grandly. "May I have a photograph of Mr. John Straker?" he demanded. The Inspector handed him one from an envelope, and armed with it, Holmes went to meet the maid.

"My horse has still not returned to me," the Colonel muttered. I was about to say something in Holmes's defense when the great detective entered the room again. "Let us visit the farm now, gentlemen," he announced. He met the stable-boy there. "Who attends to the sheep in the farm?" he asked.

"I do, sir."

"Have you noticed anything strange about them lately?"

"Three of them have gone lame, sir."

This fact pleased Holmes. "It's a long shot, Watson," he said, as we left for London. "It's a very long shot!"

Four days later, we were present for the race for the Wessex Cup. We were met by a grave looking Colonel Ross outside the stadium. "I haven't seen anything of my horse, Mr. Holmes," he stated.

"Well, Colonel, he is on the race track," Holmes replied.

"How is that possible?" the Colonel asked angrily. The reply was provided instantly as a powerful horse broke free from the enclosure, and ran past us straight into the track.

"That's Silver Blaze!" the Colonel exclaimed, excited "That's my horse! How did you do it, Mr. Holmes?"

"You shall know everything in time, Colonel," Holmes replied.

After the race was over, we made our way into the enclosure to see Silver Blaze.

"Thank you, Mr. Holmes. The horse looks fit and healthy. I do apologise for doubting your prowess. But who murdered John Straker?" the Colonel asked.

"He is right here!"

"Here? Where?"

Holmes laughed. "The murderer stands right behind you, Colonel," he stated and walked to caress the glossy neck of Silver Blaze. "The horse!" The Colonel and I exclaimed in unison. "Yes, Silver Blaze is the murderer of John Straker," Holmes declared. "However, it was an act of self-defense and John Straker was the real villain.

"Powdered opium when mixed with an ordinary dish can easily be found out. But a curry disguises the taste. It was impossible for the stranger, Fitzroy Simpson, to arrive with powdered opium the very night the dish was served. It had to be Straker and his wife! They were the only two people who

could have chosen curried mutton as supper for the night.

"The opium was added much later, after everyone else had had their food and as the dish was set aside for the stable-boy. No one else, apart from Straker and his wife had access to the dish without the maid spotting them. The silence of the dog troubled me though, as the dog did not bark during the theft, which was unusual. So, the dog knew the midnight visitor very well. The contents of Straker's pockets helped me. The knife was to serve its purpose in a delicate operation that night. Straker would use the knife to make a small cut upon the tendons of Silver Blaze's muscles. This would ensure that the horse would develop a slight lameness during the race."

"Villain!" the Colonel shouted.

"Precisely! Now let me explain why Straker did what he did. From the bills in his pocket, it was apparent that he was living a dual

life. Clearly, a lady with expensive tastes was present in his life. So, he needed money desperately. Straker wanted Silver Blaze to lose as he had betted heavily against him. I asked Mrs. Straker about the dress the bill mentioned but it had not reached her. I took down the tailor's address and visited him with Straker's photograph to discover that his name was entered as Derbyshire.

It was simple after that! Straker had led the horse to a hollow. He had picked up Simpson's tie that the latter had dropped in his flight, with the intention of maybe tying the horse's leg with it. On the moor, he had stepped behind the horse and struck a match. The horse, scared at the sudden glare, and with the natural animal instinct that some mischief was afoot, had kicked him. The steel shoe hit Straker full on the forehead and as he fell, he cut his thigh with his knife."

"Oh my God!" the Colonel exclaimed.

"I realised that Straker would not indulge in the delicate tendon-nicking without some practice," Holmes continued. "But what could he use for practice? The sheep was the obvious choice. I confirmed my assumption from the stable-boy."

"You have almost explained it all, Mr. Holmes," the Colonel explained. "Only one thing remains unanswered. Where was the horse all this time?"

"Ah, that!" Holmes replied. "The horse had bolted and one of your neighbours took care of it."

About the Author

■ Sir Arthur Ignatius Conan Doyle

Sir Arthur Ignatius Conan Doyle (22 May 1859 – 7 July 1930) was a Scottish writer and physician, famous for creating the great fictional detective called Sherlock Holmes. His stories featuring Sherlock Holmes are widely considered as milestones in the field of crime fiction.

Arthur Conan Doyle was born on 22 May, 1859, in Edinburgh, Scotland. Between 1887 and 1927, Doyle wrote four novels and fifty-six short stories featuring Sherlock Holmes, a brilliant London-based, Consulting Detective. Holmes stands out for his astute observation, deductive reasoning and forensic skills, to solve the most difficult cases. Doyle's first work featuring Sherlock Holmes and Dr. Watson was 'A Study in Scarlet.'

Conan Doyle introduced to literature the character of the 'scientific detective'. Holmes is one of the most popular characters in English literature. Not only is he a master detective, but also the epitome of the Victorian and Imperial values.

236

■ Characters

Sherlock Holmes: He is the self proclaimed consulting detective who stars in the stories. His motive for taking up a case seems to be how interesting it is and his clients range from pedestrians to royalty and even Scotland Yard. Emotionally closed off, he approaches all his social relationships based on logical thinking and deduction, practised to levels that border on fantastical. It allows him to solve the strangest cases.

Dr. Watson: Sherock Holmes's closest friend and self appointed chronicler of their exploits together, solving crimes across Britain. An ex-veteran, he becomes Holmes's friend when he shares an apartment with him at 221B, Baker Street. Eventually, he comes to know of Holmes's deep regard for him.

■ Questions

Chapter 1

- *Why did Sherlock Holmes visit Watson at midnight?*
- *Describe the conversation Sherlock Holmes had with Miss Murphy?*
- *Why was Miss Morrison reluctant to reveal the truth to Holmes?*
- *Who was the crooked man? How had he become so?*

Chapter 2

- *Who was Victor Trevor? Describe him.*
- *What did Holmes say that made Mr. Trevor faint?*
- *Who was Hudson?*
- *Why was Mr. Trevor scared of Hudson?*

Chapter 3

- *Who was Brunton? Why did he lose his job?*
- *What was the Musgrave Ritual?*
- *Why did Rachel Howell's condition alarm everyone?*
- *How did Holmes determine where the far end of the shadow of the elm would fall?*

Chapter 4

- *Why was the robbery at Acton's house strange?*
- *How did Holmes recover the missing piece of the note?*
- *Who attacked Sherlock Holmes?*
- *Why was William the coachman murdered?*

Chapter 5

- *Who was Pycroft's visitor? Describe him in detail.*
- *Briefly describe the conversation between Pycroft and his visitor.*
- *Why did Mr. Pinner try to kill himself?*
- *What breaking news did the newspaper carry?*

Chapter 6

- *Why was Grant Munro disturbed?*
- *What instructions did Holmes give to Munro?*
- *Briefly describe the events that ensued after Holmes and Watson visited Norbury.*
- *Whom did the yellow face belong to?*

Chapter 7

- *Who was Silver Blaze?*
- *What was the breaking news in London?*
- *Who had the Inspector arrested? Why?*
- *How did Straker die? Describe in detail.*